LiZZiE & LUCKY

The
Mystery
of the
**Disappearing
Rabbit**

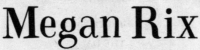

Megan Rix

Illustrated by Tim Budgen

PUFFIN

PUFFIN BOOKS

UK | USA | Canada | Ireland | Australia
India | New Zealand | South Africa

Puffin is part of the Penguin Random House group of companies
whose addresses can be found at global.penguinrandomhouse.com.

www.penguin.co.uk
www.puffin.co.uk
www.ladybird.co.uk

First published 2023

001

Text copyright © Megan Rix, 2023
Illustrations by Tim Budgen, 2023
The moral right of the author has been asserted

Set in Bembo MT Std
Text design by Janene Spencer
Printed in Great Britain by Clays Ltd, Elcograf S.p.A.

The authorized representative in the EEA is Penguin Random House Ireland,
Morrison Chambers, 32 Nassau Street, Dublin D02 YH68

A CIP catalogue record for this book is available from the British Library

ISBN: 978–0–241–59603–6

All correspondence to:
Puffin Books
Penguin Random House Children's, One Embassy Gardens
8 Viaduct Gardens, London SW11 7BW

PUFFIN BOOKS

The Mystery of the
Disappearing Rabbit

Megan Rix is the hugely popular author of animal adventure books set in the modern day and key periods of history. An animal advocate and dog-friend, Megan draws inspiration from her own adorable dogs Traffy, Bella, Freya and Ellie.

Follow Megan Rix on Twitter
@megan_rix
#LizzieandLucky

Books by Megan Rix

THE GREAT FIRE DOGS

THE BOMBER DOG

THE GREAT ESCAPE

THE VICTORY DOGS

A SOLDIER'S FRIEND

THE RUNAWAYS

ECHO COME HOME

THE HERO PUP

THE PAW HOUSE

THE LOST WAR DOG

For younger readers

ROSA AND THE DARING DOG

WINSTON AND THE MARMALADE CAT

EMMELINE AND THE PLUCKY PUP

FLORENCE AND THE MISCHIEVOUS KITTEN

Lizzie and Lucky:

THE MYSTERY OF THE MISSING PUPPIES

THE MYSTERY OF THE STOLEN TREASURE

Never forget to read to your pet

(or to someone else's)

– M.R.

To Julia, thank you x

– T.B.

WHO'S WHO

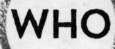

Lizzie

Lucky

Ted

Lady Azeena
and Rudy

Dad

Mum

Mr O'Keith

Bob

CHAPTER

'I just don't understand it,' Ted signed to Detective Lizzie and her assistant, Lucky, shaking his head. 'Why do Thumper and Wriggles keep escaping?' Ted used sign language rather than speaking because Lizzie was deaf. Ted loved to sign and he was really fluent in it.

Lucky, the adorable Dalmatian puppy, had learnt a lot of signs too. She knew the sign for her name and Lizzie's name, as well as 'Mum' and 'Dad'. Lizzie would often make the sign for 'Mum' or 'Dad' and then the sign for 'fetch' and Lucky would go and find them. Sometimes Lizzie's mum or dad wanted Lucky to fetch Lizzie instead. Lucky liked being helpful and she enjoyed learning new signs. Her current favourite ones were 'Lizzie', 'food', 'toys' and 'play'.

They weren't playing now though. It was a sunny Saturday afternoon and Lizzie and Lucky were helping their friend, Ted, to solve a mystery.

Inside their hutch, peeping out, were Ted's two rabbits called Thumper and Wriggles. Lucky wagged her tail, but the rabbits didn't want to be friends with the puppy. Thumper thumped her back paw on the floor of the hutch to tell Lucky to go away. But Lucky only sat down and tilted her head to one side with one ear up and one ear down, confused.

The first thing Lizzie needed to do was thoroughly inspect the rabbits' hutch. She pulled a torch from her detective's bag so she could look into every nook and cranny. Ted had texted her to say he'd found Wriggles and Thumper out of their hutch and hopping about on the lawn that morning. It was the third time they'd escaped this week.

Lizzie wanted to investigate how they were getting out. Lucky helped by sniffing all around the hutch to see if she could smell the rabbits' scent and trace their paw prints. But despite all her searching, Lizzie couldn't find any rabbit-sized escape holes to explain their disappearance and, for all Lucky's sniffing, she couldn't tell where

they were headed when they did get out.
It was *still* a mystery.

'The rescue centre didn't tell me that
Thumper and Wriggles were escape
artists!' Ted signed, looking sad. 'I thought
they were happy living here, but now they
only want to run away. I haven't even
seen them do a binky once.'

Lizzie knew how much Ted wanted his
rabbits to feel settled and content. When
rabbits were truly happy, they sometimes
did a playful twisting leap of joy in mid-air
called **a binky.**

'Not a single one!' Ted added for
emphasis.

Lucky picked up her favourite octopus
toy and started playfully throwing it in

the air. Her tail wagged and wagged as she pounced on the toy. Seeing Lucky so happy gave Lizzie a good idea that might just solve Ted's mystery.

'We'll make your garden so much fun that Thumper and Wriggles won't want to disappear from it!' she signed to Ted.

Ted thought this was a great idea, but he looked at his watch and frowned. 'The only problem is it's not long till the magic contest,' he signed.

But Lizzie thought they'd have just enough time to make an adventure garden for the rabbits before they left . . .

THINGS A RABBIT ADVENTURE GARDEN NEEDS:

1. Hidden tasty treats

2. Surprise digging spots

3. Obstacles

4. New toys to play with

Lizzie and Ted started digging. Lucky came running over with her octopus toy and dropped it in the hole.

'Oh no, Lucky. You might lose it if you drop it in there,' Ted said.

Lucky tilted her head to one side as if

she was listening to Ted and then leant into the hole and retrieved her octopus toy, leaving it on the grass. She ran over to the rabbits' twine ball lying nearby and picked that up instead.

'Don't break it, Lucky. Rabbit toys aren't as strong as dog toys,' Ted told her.

Lucky picked up the ball with her teeth, being careful not to bite too hard, then dropped it into the hole. Now the rabbits could have fun digging around and finding it.

Then Lizzie tied a carrot top with lots of green leaves to a low branch of a bush. Lucky got to eat some carrot too. It was delicious!

Thumper and Wriggles mostly ate hay,

so Lizzie made a tray of it for them to dig in.

Ted ran inside the house, where Lizzie's mum and dad were drinking tea with his gran. He came back out again with some courgettes and peppers. 'Rabbits like these and they're good for them too,' he signed. 'But we can't give them too much. Hay is supposed to be their main food.'

They wanted Thumper and Wriggles to be excited when they found the little treats – but not so full up that they could barely move.

Lucky ran back to the hutch to check how the rabbits were doing. But Thumper only stamped her paw again, while Wriggles hid behind a toy when he saw her. Lucky sat down in front of the hutch and gave a low whine. *Why didn't they want to be friends?*

She ran over to the rabbits' twine ball again and took it out of the hole. It wasn't long before Lucky was pushing it across the grass with her nose, then lying on her back and rolling on it. Very soon it was squashed and not very ball-shaped.

Lizzie and Ted laughed as they watched her rolling.

'Lucky really loves playing with toys,' Ted signed and Lizzie nodded. Lucky really did and she had lots at home, but they were only taking one with them to the theatre today.

'That's it for now,' Lizzie signed at last. There were carrot tops and bits of parsley and lots of hay for the rabbits to munch on all around the garden.

'Wow!' said Ted as they admired their hard work. The garden looked much more exciting for Thumper and Wriggles now.

'They can jump over that,' Lizzie signed, pointing to the mini-fence they'd made. 'They could go under it too or round the side.'

As well as tasty food for the rabbits, they'd put out a tray for digging in and empty cardboard rolls for them to find and chew on.

Ted grinned and opened the door to the rabbits' hutch. There was just time for Thumper and Wriggles to have a little play before the magic contest. Ted had made a special ramp that led from the hutch to the grass. He put the ramp in place for them to hop down.

Lizzie and Lucky stood back so the rabbits wouldn't be scared. But Thumper and Wriggles didn't come out. They stayed firmly in their hutch.

Ted lifted Thumper out of the hutch and Lizzie told Lucky to sit and stay before she lifted Wriggles out. Wriggles was very wriggly!

'Careful not to hold him on his back like a baby,' Ted said as Lizzie lipread. 'It's bad for rabbits' hearts. They think they've been caught by a predator and they freeze and play dead!'

Lizzie put Wriggles down on the grass and Ted placed Thumper on the grass too. Lucky put out a paw but she stayed sitting as Lizzie had told her to.

'Does freezing work?' Lizzie signed. 'Would a fox let go of a rabbit if it played dead?'

Ted shrugged. 'I'm not sure but it's what

a rabbit would do in the wild if a fox caught it and it couldn't get away. The lady at the animal rescue centre said pretending to be dead is called tonic immobility and it's bad for rabbits' hearts. Did you know a group of wild rabbits is called **a fluffle**?'

Lizzie shook her head, and made the sign for **'cute'**.

'Dogs don't like being carried on their backs either,' she signed. 'They don't feel safe. Of course, it's different when Lucky rolls on one of her toys or wants a tummy rub!'

Ted grinned. 'I don't think my rabbits would like a belly rub,' he signed. 'They don't even really like being picked up.

They'd probably run away – oh no!'

Ted pointed at Thumper and Wriggles.
The rabbits were running back up the
ramp and into their hutch.

'Thumper and Wriggles will probably
play in their adventure garden when
Lucky's not around,' Lizzie signed to Ted.
She knew Lucky wanted to be friends
with the rabbits, but Thumper and
Wriggles just didn't feel the same way.

Ted nodded. 'I hope so. I want them to
have fun,' he signed. 'Like Gobbler and
Jaws.'

Lizzie held up two thumbs. She wanted
that too. Gobbler and Jaws were Ted's two
rats. They'd also come from the rescue
centre. It had all sorts of animals and pets

looking for new homes.

Lizzie made the sign for 'come' to Lucky and the puppy ran over straight away.

Just then, Lizzie's mum and dad came outside with Ted's gran. Mum was wearing a starry scarf and wand-decorated hearing aids for the magic contest.

Once they'd admired the rabbits' new adventure garden, Lizzie's dad pointed to his watch.

Lizzie beckoned to Ted's gran. She wanted her to come with them too, but Ted's gran shook her head. She'd had a fall in the street a few weeks ago and she didn't want to go out now. 'What if I fall again?' she said as Lizzie lipread.

'We won't let you fall,' Lizzie's mum and dad signed, and Ted translated. But Ted's gran still shook her head.

'Well, if you're sure. We'll tell you all about it when we get back,' Ted said.

Lizzie clipped Lucky's lead to her collar. It was time for the magic contest!

CHAPTER 2

Lucky trotted along on her lead beside Lizzie and sniffed at interesting smells on the way to the theatre where Mum and Dad worked. It was only a ten-minute walk, but they wanted to arrive early in case any last-minute scenery painting or prop repairs needed to be done before the magic contest.

Lucky had been to the theatre lots of times. Lizzie's mum and dad would never leave her alone when they went to work

because they knew she'd be lonely.
Fortunately, the theatre manager loved
dogs and was happy for Lucky to be there.
If Mum and Dad were working at the
weekends, then Lizzie came to the theatre
too. Lucky loved it most of all when Lizzie
was there.

They were halfway to the theatre
when Lizzie realized she hadn't picked
up Lucky's octopus toy. It was still lying
forgotten in Ted's garden, along with her
detective's bag. Lucky loved playing with
her octopus toy but it was too late to go
back for it – or her bag – now.

It was time to see what tricks the magicians would perform! Lizzie was looking forward to working out how they were done. Most people couldn't spot the magicians' tricks but Lizzie sometimes could. There was a saying – *The quickness of the hand deceives the eye* – but Lizzie was ready. She was determined not to be fooled.

'I hope Thumper and Wriggles don't get out of their hutch while we're out,' Ted signed, shaking his head.

'Thumper and Wriggles are really good at escaping,' Lizzie told her mum and dad.

'Like Houdini,' signed Dad with a smile as he took Lizzie's hand in his giant-sized one. 'He was the greatest escape artist in the world.'

Lizzie grinned up at him. Dad loved the famous magician, who'd lived a long, long time ago – lots of Deaf people did. Houdini was said to have learnt both British and American sign language and used them when he performed for Deaf audiences. Not many hearing magicians had ever done that!

'Houdini was a great magician and showman and escape artist,' Dad signed, and Lizzie nodded. 'The first time he performed, he was only nine years old. He did a trapeze act and was known as the *Prince of the Air.*'

'It's rumoured that he once performed

at our local theatre back in the early nineteen hundreds,' Mum added.

'I would have loved to see him perform,' signed Dad.

'Me too,' signed Ted. 'But I'm really looking forward to seeing the *Astonishing Lady Azeena and her Amazing Animals* this afternoon.'

Lizzie nodded in agreement. She was excited about seeing Lady Azeena too. Lady Azeena was a magician who was deaf and used sign language. She was very important to the Deaf community – a role model, in fact, as well as being an amazing magician.

'It's the first time she's performed her new act and she's chosen our theatre for

Astonishing Lady Azeena and her Amazing Animals

the premiere,' Mum signed. 'It's such an honour. They say that before she got her rabbit, Rudy, she was going to give up magic. She hasn't performed for ages.'

'Are there any other magicians who are deaf in the magic contest?' Ted wanted to know.

Dad shrugged. 'I don't think so. No one who uses sign language, anyway.'

'There could be some deaf magicians in the contest who don't use sign language,' Mum added. Not everyone who was deaf knew how to sign. Most people didn't. Lizzie's mum thought this was a shame and Lizzie did too. Sign language was so beautiful and she wanted everyone to know how to use it.

Lucky pulled ahead as they turned the corner into the street the theatre was on. In front of them they saw a large lorry being unloaded. It was blocking the road outside the theatre and holding up traffic on both sides.

'Quick,' signed Lizzie, and they all hurried to see what was happening. Lucky's little nose sniffed the air and she gave an excited, high-pitched **woof**.

Four people were unloading two big black metal trunks with **Beware Dangerous Animals** painted in white letters on the sides. Lucky was very interested in the tall trunks and wagged her tail, sniffing the air again as she tried to pull Lizzie towards them. But Lizzie didn't think they should get too close.

As well as the white writing, the trunks displayed the skull and crossbones symbol for danger – plus an exclamation mark on a yellow background with the words **Danger – Wild Animals** underneath. The black metal containers had lots of padlocks on them too, but no gaps for the dangerous animals to look out of or for people to see in through.

Lizzie bit her bottom lip and made the sign for 'not right'. It would be pitch-dark inside those trunks. It wasn't fair that the animals didn't have any light, or that they couldn't even see out, no matter how dangerous they were.

Lucky looked up at Lizzie, then at the trunks . . . and whined.

At the sound of car horns honking, Ted looked round. He grinned and pretended to be honking a car horn to Lizzie so she

28

would understand what he'd heard. Lizzie laughed and nudged her mum. Then Mum gave Dad a nudge, pointed to the cars and imitated pressing a car horn too. Lizzie's dad loved tooting the horn on their car whenever he got the chance. He didn't care that it was too loud for hearing people or that they didn't like it. He liked it and could hear it.

At that moment, a golden stretch limousine swerved past the other traffic and drew up to the pavement in front of the theatre. Now the road was even more blocked! A man wearing a tuxedo, bow tie and top hat jumped out and ran round to open the back passenger door.

Lizzie watched as a lady with lots

of rings on her fingers, wearing a long golden cape with stars on the back of it and fur round the collar, appeared from the car. At first, Lizzie thought it might be *real* animal fur and she gave a shudder because she didn't like the idea of animals being hurt just to make clothes. But then the fur opened its eyes, its ears pricked up and Lizzie gasped. It was a rabbit!

'Houdini had a rabbit,' Lizzie's dad signed. 'A great big rabbit! It was mostly white with some black spots, a black nose and black circles round its eyes. Plus, it had black ears and a black line running along its back'

Lucky looked up at the rabbit and wagged her tail.

The man who'd opened the car door quickly got back in the vehicle and drove it towards the car park next to the theatre. The lady in the golden cape with the rabbit – now sitting on her shoulder – stood waiting.

Ted nudged Lizzie. 'That's the *Astonishing Lady Azeena*!' he signed, indicating the woman wearing the long cape. 'And that's Rudy.' Ted pointed at the white rabbit. 'He's famous.'

'And named after the legendary Houdini's pet rabbit, who was also called Rudy,' Dad signed. 'Although the two rabbits don't look the same at all.'

'I can't believe Lady Azeena is so close,' signed Ted. 'Do you think those are real emeralds and diamonds and rubies in her rings?'

Lizzie's mum shrugged. It was hard to tell.

'Do you think I could get her autograph?' Ted signed.

'Maybe,' signed Lizzie's dad. 'You could always ask.'

Ted was about to do so when Lizzie saw Dot, one of the young volunteer stagehands, come running out of the theatre's entrance. Lizzie and Lucky had met her before at the theatre. Dot was sixteen and always wore a paw-print necklace that Lizzie liked very much.

Dot stopped in front of Lady Azeena and pointed at the big metal trunks with the padlocks on them.

Lady Azeena shrugged and shook her head. She looked towards the car park where her driver had gone. In the next moment, he came hurrying back over as Lady Azeena beckoned to him and then pointed at Dot.

There was a conversation between the man and Dot, during which Lizzie saw Dot pointing at the metal trunks again.

The man nodded and signed to Lady Azeena. She looked angry, shaking her head, then signed back to him. Lizzie, her mum, dad and Ted could all easily understand what they were signing.

The man nodded again and then said something to Dot. Ted, who was also watching, translated for Lizzie and her mum and dad. 'Lady Azeena says she knows what's best for them. Although Rudy might like some water. He has a special porcelain bowl, that was made especially for him, that he drinks out of. Make sure the water isn't too cold, though. He only likes tepid water.'

Dot pointed at the two big trunks on the pavement again. She looked worried. 'Those animals will be thirsty too,' she said.

The man used sign language to translate Dot's words to Lady Azeena.

'It's not fair,' Dot continued. 'They need

a drink. I'd be happy to get them some water.'

Lizzie frowned as she watched Lady Azeena shaking her head. Lizzie agreed with Dot. The animals *did* need a drink. They were all shocked at Lady Azeena's heartlessness. This wasn't the right way to treat performing animals, or any animals for that matter – locking them up, keeping them in the dark and not even giving them any water.

Lizzie thought Lady Azeena should at least let the animals have a drink, and if the poor creatures were anything like Lucky, which they probably were, they'd like a snack too. She looked down at her puppy with a frown . . . and then gasped.

Where had Lucky got that?

The puppy now had a toy in her mouth. It was a soft, smiling silver star. Lucky bit down on it and Ted signed to Lizzie that the toy squeaked.

Lizzie looked round but no one seemed to be missing a toy. She had no idea

where Lucky had found it or who it really belonged to. Perhaps a child had dropped it, but she couldn't see any other children and besides, it wasn't necessarily a child's toy. It could be the plaything of a dog or even a cat. Did it belong to one of the dangerous animals in the metal trunks? Wouldn't they have ripped it up?

Lizzie looked over at Dot, who seemed really unhappy. She was shaking her head in dismay as she watched Lady Azeena, Rudy the rabbit and Lady Azeena's assistant enter the theatre.

Lizzie, her mum and dad and Ted watched the black metal trunks that were now being wheeled up the ramp and into the theatre. **It just wasn't**

right! The animals inside them were so traumatized, Ted signed, that they didn't even make a sound.

Lucky looked up at Lizzie, then shook her new silver star toy, which made another squeak. But inside the trunks there was silence.

CHAPTER 3

Lizzie couldn't stop thinking about Lady Azeena's poor mistreated animals as they made their way into the theatre. Lucky had her new silver smiling star toy in her mouth. She seemed really happy with it. But she'd have to give it up when they found its real owner.

In the foyer of the theatre, Mum and Dad pointed to a life-sized poster of Houdini. He had dark curly hair and an intense stare.

'Houdini was born in Hungary but went to live in America when he was four,' Dad signed.

The poster had a picture frame made of metal chains and padlocks.

'We made the frame,' Mum signed to Lizzie.

'Houdini was known as the *King of Handcuffs*,' Dad added. 'He could escape from anything!'

Lucky threw her smiling silver star toy up in the air and then pounced on it.

'Did Houdini have any brothers and sisters?' Ted wanted to know.

Lizzie's dad nodded. 'He had lots – one half-brother, four brothers and a sister. One of his brothers was also a magician and escape artist. Houdini called him "Dash".'

Lizzie grinned and signed, 'Dash is a good name for an escape artist.'

Just then, a man wearing a suit and a spotted bow tie appeared. He didn't look happy at all when he saw Lucky. 'No dogs allowed!' he said as Lizzie lipread. He put his hands out to stop Lizzie and Lucky from going any further into the theatre.

'But there are animals already in the show. The *Astonishing Lady Azeena* has lots of them,' said Ted. 'We've just seen them being unloaded.'

'That's different,' said the man. 'Those animals are in the performance.'

'Who are you?' signed Dad, and Ted translated.

The man said he was Mr O'Keith, the temporary theatre manager.

'Where's Jenny, the permanent manager?' Mum signed. 'Jenny always lets Lucky in. Lucky's been here many times before and there's never been a problem.'

Lizzie wished Jenny was there. She liked her very much. Jenny was even trying to learn some sign language, with Lizzie's help. Lizzie had taught Jenny to sign the letters of her name, plus 'hello' and 'goodbye' – but they were only really a wave.

Lucky liked Jenny too, because she often brought along something tasty for her to eat.

'Jenny's busy today,' Mr O'Keith said.

There was something about his face and body language that made Lizzie think he was lying. *What was going on? What was he trying to hide?*

'I'm in charge today, so it's my rules and I say no dogs,' he continued.

Lucky picked up the silver star toy and dropped it at the man's feet. Mr O'Keith promptly kicked it away. Lucky pounced on it again. She sat down and looked at the manager with the toy in her mouth, ready for a game. But Mr O'Keith only scowled.

They all told him that Lucky was a
really well-behaved puppy and wouldn't
cause any trouble. But he only looked
more angry and kept shaking his head.

Lizzie was really worried. Then Mrs
Rose, who lived next door to Ted, arrived.
She had Victor, her hearing dog, with her
and he was wearing his special hearing-
dog coat. Mrs Rose had only become
deaf a little while ago and had a cochlear
implant to help her to hear. She hadn't
been learning how to sign for very long
and she wasn't as good as Ted.

Victor wagged his tail when he saw
Lizzie. She often took him for a walk and
Victor liked walks very much, especially
when they were with his friend Lucky.

Lucky and Victor sniffed noses, and
then Lucky dropped her new toy in front
of Victor so he could have a look at it.
Once Victor had given the smiling silver

star a sniff, Lucky picked it up again.

When Mrs Rose heard that Lucky wasn't being allowed into the theatre, she wasn't pleased at all. She said that although Lucky wasn't a hearing dog like Victor, she could be one in training and was already helping Lizzie in all sorts of ways. Legally, the theatre had to allow all assistance dogs inside. It wouldn't look good to ban a puppy that was being so helpful, especially one who had previously been allowed inside many times. 'What would the papers think?' she asked as Lizzie lipread. Mrs Rose had a fierce expression on her face.

Now Mr O'Keith looked worried. He gave a big sigh and finally agreed that

Lucky could come inside. 'But you can't sit with the main audience,' he said grudgingly. 'Someone might have dog allergies.'

This didn't make sense at all because he was allowing Victor to sit with the audience, but Lizzie didn't care where she and Lucky sat. All she wanted was for Lucky to be

allowed to come inside. She didn't want to watch the magic contest without her puppy and she would never ever think of leaving her behind.

'I promise Lucky will be good,' Lizzie signed, and Ted translated for the theatre manager, who didn't look like he believed him at all.

'Just make sure it doesn't get dog hairs on the seats or have an *accident*,' Mr O'Keith said. 'I don't want any mess in this theatre.'

'Where are the *Astonishing Lady Azeena*'s animals being kept?' Ted asked. He thought they were much more likely to make messes – probably all over the metal cabinets in which they were imprisoned.

'They're staying where they are, in their trunks, until the *Astonishing Lady Azeena's* act – apart from that rabbit, of course,' Mr O'Keith told Ted. 'It goes everywhere with her. Probably has it's own special seat in that golden limousine of hers. Spoilt, I say, and it probably has fleas. Does *your* dog have fleas?' The theatre manager pointed at Lucky.

Lizzie lipread the word **'fleas'** and shook her head vigorously. She wished Jenny the permanent manager was there instead. She didn't like Mr O'Keith at all . . . and what's more, she didn't trust him. All of her detective instincts were warning her against him.

Dad frowned. 'But Lady Azeena is almost the last act in the contest. That's a *really* long time for those animals to be cooped up in the dark,' he signed, and Ted translated.

Lizzie nodded. It *was* a really long time. Especially since they'd already been stuck in those metal trunks in the lorry on the drive here.

Mr O'Keith just shrugged. 'Not my problem,' he said as he headed off.

Lizzie and Ted told Mrs Rose what had happened with Lady Azeena's animals.

'I'm not sure I like Lady Azeena very much now,' Ted said. 'I feel so sorry for her poor animals – apart from Rudy, of course.'

Lizzie nodded because she felt the same way. Even the great Houdini wouldn't have been able to escape from those padlocked trunks.

Something needed to be DONE.

CHAPTER 4

Now that Lucky was allowed into the
theatre, Lizzie, Lucky and Ted followed
Lizzie's mum and dad along the corridor
and down some steps to the green room,
where the magicians were relaxing before
the contest.

'Why's it called a *green* room when it
isn't even green?' Ted wanted to know. The
walls were a dull creamy white colour.

'It's just what they've always been
called,' signed Dad.

'I've never been to a theatre where the green room was green,' signed Mum.

'Weird,' signed Lizzie.

Lady Azeena and her rabbit, Rudy, were in the green room along with the other contestants. Lizzie watched a man wearing a sparkly costume doing

stretching exercises against a wall. Next to him was a woman juggling. A bald man was looking in a mirror as he carefully positioned a green wig on his head. Another man put a set of vampire teeth inside his mouth as a lady carrying a bundle of swords squeezed past him.

Everyone, apart from Lady Azeena, was laughing and chatting together. The other contestants all seemed to be people who could hear and didn't know any sign language. It felt like they were all friends already. But not friends with Lady Azeena.

Ted put his hands to his ears and signed to Lizzy that the room was very noisy.

Lizzie signed back that she could feel the excitement in the air. The magicians were probably nervous as well as excited. Only Lady Azeena seemed icily calm as she slowly stroked Rudy. Lizzie looked at the big rings on some of her fingers and thought they must be heavy to wear. Rudy had moved into Lady Azeena's lap and was munching a small bunch of parsley.

'Thumper and Wriggles like parsley too,' Ted signed to Lizzie. 'And thyme and mint. Whenever they eat mint, they smell like they've just cleaned their teeth!'

Lizzie thought Rudy looked very happy – Lady Azeena did seem to love him very much.

Lizzie had let go of Lucky's lead without thinking and now Lucky was very interested in Rudy. She wagged her tail as she trotted towards the big rabbit.

Ted wanted to ask Lady Azeena for her autograph on a piece of paper he'd found, so was standing close by. As Lucky continued her approach, he began to feel worried that Rudy would be scared of Lucky, like Thumper and Wriggles were.

'**Sorry,**' he signed to Lazy Azeena,
as he gently pushed Lucky back towards
Lizzy.

Lucky looked up at him and then back
at Rudy.

'You can sign?' Lady Azeena signed to
Ted, seeming surprised.

Ted nodded and pointed to Lizzie and her mum and dad.

'Yes – Lizzie, her parents and I all use sign language,' he signed as Lizzie came to join him.

Lady Azeena smiled. 'I'm so pleased there are more people here who know sign language besides me and my assistant, Bob,' she signed. Then she added, 'You can let the puppy go, you know. Rudy's not frightened of dogs.'

'Lucky's got a hearing-dog friend called Victor, who's also here,' Lizzie signed.

'Animals can make such a difference to a person's life,' Lady Azeena signed back and Lizzie nodded. 'Before Rudy came to live with me I was going to give up magic.'

'Why?' Ted signed, his eyes wide.

'I had such bad stage fright. I felt sick all the time and my hands wouldn't stop shaking,' Lady Azeena told him. 'It got so bad it was impossible for me to perform. But then Rudy arrived and as long as he's on stage with me, my stage fright goes away.'

Mum and Dad had joined them now. 'So that's why you didn't perform for such a long time?' Mum signed.

Lady Azeena nodded. 'Without Rudy, I couldn't be a magician. If I didn't have him, I don't know what I'd do. He's helped me so much.'

'Like a therapy rabbit,' signed Dad.

Lady Azeena nodded again. 'Rabbits

are often used as therapy animals,' she signed back.

'We have a reading therapy dog that visits our school on Wednesdays,' Ted said. 'Children get to read to her.'

'Do you think there are reading rabbits?' signed Lizzie. She thought it'd be brilliant to read to a rabbit.

Lucky looked up and wagged her tail. Lizzie read stories to her already.

'Rabbits like being read to – it lets them build up trust with a person slowly. Some animal rescue centres even have reading-to-rabbit schemes,' Lady Azeena signed.

Ted's nose wrinkled. 'I don't know if Wriggles and Thumper would like that,' he signed.

63

Lady Azeena signed back that he could give it a try and see how it went.

Dot came over with some water for Rudy. It was in his special porcelain bowl with his name on it.

Lady Azeena pointed to the floor near Rudy and Dot put it down, then her assistant, Bob, came back and thanked Dot.

'What about Lady Azeena's other animals?' the stagehand said as Lizzie lipread.

'Don't worry about them,' Bob told her.

But Dot's face looked like she was worried, and Lizzie was worried too.

'Pizza!' said Ted, as a girl who looked a lot like Dot came into the room and piled lots of boxes from the local Plant Pizza restaurant on to a table.

'Compliments of Lady Azeena,' Bob told everyone in a big loud voice. 'Please help yourselves. There's plenty to go round.'

Lizzie noticed the Plant Pizza girl's name tag, which said Ann. Ann and Dot exchanged a look as she put the last of the pizza boxes down on the table. The two girls looked so alike that Lizzie was sure they must be related. Everyone immediately started swarming round and helping themselves to the food.

A moment later, Mr O'Keith came into the room and stuck two handwritten notices to the wall:

Please don't leave greasy fingermarks!

Please throw all litter away in the correct bins.

Dad looked at Lizzie and rolled his eyes. Lizzie quickly put her hand up to her mouth so Mr O'Keith wouldn't see her laugh. The theatre manager was a pest, but Dad was so funny!

'Yum,' Ted said as he bit into a large slice of Plant Pizza's famous meat-free-pepperoni-style pizza.

Lucky loved Plant Pizzas – especially pepperoni flavour – and Lizzie shared her slice with the puppy.

The only people not eating pizza were Mr O'Keith, Dot and Ann. They were over in one corner of the room. Lizzie couldn't lipread what Mr O'Keith was saying because his back was to her. Their heads were close together, but Lizzie saw him pointing at Lady Azeena and the two girls nodding. Then he swung round and pointed straight at Lizzie and Lucky. The puppy nudged her head against Lizzie, and they looked at each other. Something was definitely not right.

CHAPTER 5

Ten minutes later the alarm bell on the wall flashed. It was nearly time for the magic contest to begin.

'Audience members, please take your seats,' Mr O'Keith said. Then the bossy theatre manager escorted Lizzie and Lucky past most of the seats, which all had a programme on them. Mum, Dad and Ted followed. They went almost to the front of the theatre . . . but then far over to the left side, away from everyone else. Mr O'Keith pointed to a rickety wooden chair, partially hidden by a pillar. It didn't have a very good view, but you could see the wings at the left side of the stage behind the curtains. The wings were where the magicians waited for their turn to come on and the stagehands got the props ready.

Lizzie liked the fact that they were seated there. It was different. But Dad didn't like it at all. He looked cross.

'She can't see properly,' he signed to Mr O'Keith and Ted translated for him.

'It's OK,' Lizzie signed. 'I don't mind.' It was the perfect seat for a detective to sit in.

Dad didn't agree. 'No. It's not fair. I'll sit there with Lucky and you sit with Mum and Ted, Lizzie.'

But Lizzie shook her head. 'It's fine,' she signed. 'I'll be fine. I would like a programme, though.'

'She doesn't even have a programme,' Ted said to Mr O'Keith, and the temporary theatre manager sighed loudly, pulled a tatty looking one from his pocket and gave it to Lizzie.

Lizzie made the sign for **'thank you'**. She was glad she had a programme because it meant she could see what each of the acts was going to be.

Lucky wagged her tail at Mr O'Keith, but he only waved his hands as if he was trying to shoo her away. Lizzie thought he must *really* not like dogs!

Ted, Mum and Dad asked to sit with

her, but the manager shook his head. 'The rest of you must sit in the seated area. Fire regulations.'

Dad looked like he wanted to argue again but Lizzie shook her head.

She watched Ted and her parents eventually take their seats in the auditorium as close to her as they could. Lizzie waved and they waved back. She was going to make the best of it.

The lights went down and a few moments later, Lizzie felt a gentle tap on her arm that made her jump. It was Ted!

Luckily, there was enough room for them both to fit on the chair. But it was a bit of a squeeze when Lucky wanted to get on too!

The stage curtains opened. It was time for the first act.

Lizzie and Ted were really excited. They'd been looking forward to the contest for ages. Lucky was excited too. She was sitting on Lizzie's lap now and gave her face a quick lick.

They could all see the stage – not perfectly but well enough. And, unlike everyone else, they had a good view of the wings. Best of all, the bossy theatre manager was nowhere about.

The first magician was the man dressed as a wacky professor with lots of green frizzy hair. It said in the programme that he was a 'sand magician'. Lizzie had never even heard of a sand magician before and she'd certainly never seen one in action. She was very interested. All of her family and most of her friends loved watching magic because it was so visual. It didn't even matter too much if the magicians didn't know any sign language because you could see what was happening.

First, the sand magician pointed to a crystal bowl on a small table. Beside it were three oversized test tubes in a wooden stand with different-coloured sand in each of them — red, green and blue. The sand magician picked up a glass of water and showed it to the audience before taking a swig from it. He then poured the rest of the water into the crystal bowl. The magician was talking the whole time but Lizzie didn't need to lipread him to understand what was happening. All she needed to do was watch.

Next, the magician picked up his wand and stirred the water around with it, while at the same time waving his other hand about – and the water turned from clear to black. Lizzie frowned. How had that happened? The magician picked up the big test tube of green sand and poured it into the bowl of water. He did the same with the red and blue sand. Once they were all in the bowl and the test tubes were empty, he stirred them together with his wand. Finally, he put his hand into the bowl and scooped up each colour of sand. Amazingly, the colours hadn't all turned

into a mess of brown like they would if you mixed red, green and blue paint. The sands were now red, green and blue once again.

Finally, the sand magician stirred the water and it turned from black to clear once again.

Lizzie, Ted and the rest of the audience clapped and clapped.

When the lights came on, Lucky jumped off the seat while Lizzie and Ted stood up and made the sign for **'fantastic'** to Lizzie's mum and dad, who were holding their thumbs up.

The first act had been amazing, and Lizzie and Ted were very much looking forward to the next one. But at that moment their view was blocked by Mr O'Keith. He started waggling one finger at them and Lizzie was able to lipread him.

'Any more disobedience and you will be thrown out – and **banned** from this theatre!'

Ted looked panicked and hurried back

to his own seat as Mr O'Keith stomped off.

Lizzie gave a **big sigh**. It would have been more fun having Ted there. But Mr O'Keith had been too angry to disobey. She thought back to Mr O'Keith, Dot and Ann in the green room. She wished she'd been able to lipread them from where she had been standing.

Lizzie began to tap her chin and reminded Lucky that they needed to be on the lookout for any other strange activity.

*

When the lights went down again, Lucky hopped back on to Lizzie's lap on the rickety old seat. Lizzie was glad she couldn't see Mr O'Keith anywhere as they waited for the second act to start. He probably wouldn't like the puppy sitting on her lap.

Next there was an escape artist who chose Lizzie's dad to come up on stage to help him. Dad checked the padlocks to make sure they worked properly and held both thumbs up once he'd done so. The escape artist thanked him in sign language before climbing inside the sack. Dad secured the padlocks at the top.

Dad waved to Lizzie at the end of the act and signed, **'Almost as good as Houdini!'**

Lizzie remembered Dad telling her how Houdini had performed the same act but usually in much more dangerous situations. More than once, he'd escaped while being hung over dangerous cliffs or after being thrown into a rushing river.

Lizzie held her thumbs up to her dad. That was one of the brilliant things about sign language – you could sign from far away and still be understood, as long as the other person could see you.

After the escapologist, there was
a magician with an ancient-looking
wooden container known as a
transformation box. First, the magician
opened the box to show the audience it
was empty. Then he opened each side,
one after the other, so everyone could be
absolutely sure. The lining was covered
in green and white stripes.

The magician gave a smile, closed
the box and waved his wand over it . . .
and when he opened it again, it was full
of jewels. Then he shut the box, and on
opening it the next time – it was empty.
Incredible! thought Lizzie.

Next was a magician who levitated her
assistant above the floor. Then a comedy

magician, dressed as a clown, who pulled roses from behind Mrs Rose's ear and gave them to her with a little salute.

Lucky hopped off Lizzie's lap and started rolling on her back on top of her new toy. Lizzie looked round to see if grumpy Mr O'Keith was watching but she couldn't see him anywhere. Good.

For the next act, a magician put her assistant in a tall cabinet with holes in it, bolted the door shut and then put swords through the holes! When the cabinet was opened, the assistant had disappeared. But then a spotlight swept over the auditorium seats in an arch. When the spotlight stopped, it shone on the assistant, who was now standing at the back of the theatre.

It was a really good trick
and everyone clapped loudly.
Some people even stood up to clap.

Detective Lizzie thought it was good
too, but she'd worked out how it was done
and couldn't wait to tell Ted!

Then, a magician dressed as Dracula appeared on stage in a cloud of red smoke. It looked very dramatic, but from where Lizzie was sitting she could see the red smoke billowing from a smoke machine that Dot was working.

Lucky didn't like the red smoke and Lizzie saw her sneeze. Lizzie sniffed too but she couldn't smell anything. Lucky gave a little shudder. Her puppy nose was very sensitive and it had often helped with their detective work in the past.

Then, finally, it was the turn of the **Astonishing Lady Azeena and her Amazing Animals!**

CHAPTER 6

The stage curtains opened slowly and the spotlight shone on Rudy. The rabbit was sitting on a velvet cushion atop a small table, a giant carrot chew toy under one of his paws. He stared out at the audience and was the only one on stage for what felt like a very long time, but Lizzie knew it was probably only about thirty seconds.

From where she sat, Lizzie could see the metal trunks containing Lady Azeena's dangerous animals. The creatures were waiting in the wings – still padlocked inside the containers. No one seemed to be paying them any attention, although Lizzie could see Bob standing close by.

She frowned as she thought about the mysterious dangerous animals that Lady Azeena had brought with her. How could she love Rudy so much and be so kind to him when she treated her other animals so badly? And anyway, why would Lady Azeena even want to keep dangerous animals when she had Rudy? Wouldn't the rabbit be at risk while they were around? Surely Lady Azeena would be worried about that? Maybe that was why she locked them up . . . but the more Lizzie thought about it, the odder it seemed. If she'd had her detective's bag and it hadn't been dark in the theatre, she would have written a list of possible solutions. Instead, she ran through the alternatives in her head.

What sort of animal didn't mind being locked in the dark and didn't need to drink?

When you've eliminated the impossible, whatever remains, however improbable, must be the truth, as the great detective Sherlock Holmes would say. In other words, when the impossible solutions are crossed off your list, the only one left, however unlikely, must be the right one!

Lizzie smiled to herself and Lucky wagged her tail. Now she understood. It was all perfectly clear.

Just then, a thick cloud of golden smoke filled the stage. Lizzie knew it came from the smoke machine, but she thought she saw a shadow darting about too. When the smoke cleared the *Astonishing Lady Azeena* was standing in the centre of the stage. Lizzie knew she must have come up through the hidden trapdoor.

She knew about it because Dad had pointed the trapdoor out to her when he'd shown her the hole that was supposed to have been made so the water could drain away after Houdini's water trick. Both Mum and Dad were convinced that the hole was proof Houdini had once performed at their theatre.

Lizzie remembered Dad explaining it to her in sign language. *Every theatre Houdini performed in had a hole like that in the stage so the water inside the glass case he was escaping from had somewhere to go. Four stagehands would be positioned underneath the stage, holding a giant waterproof sheet to catch the water.* Then he'd added that he wished he could have been one of those stagehands.

Now Lizzie saw the audience clapping and she was about to clap too when she realized something was wrong. Rudy wasn't on stage any more . . . the rabbit had disappeared! All that was left was Rudy's carrot chew, lying on the floor.

For a brief second Lizzie thought maybe it could be part of the act. Was it just an illusion? But then Lady Azeena screamed in horror as she stared and pointed at the empty space where Rudy had been. Lady Azeena's scream was so loud that even Lizzie could hear it. This couldn't be part of her magic act – the sound was too desperate.

This was real.

CHAPTER 7

Lady Azeena began looking all around the stage in total panic. Her hands shook as she threw props about in the search for her rabbit, Rudy. Then she went running off the stage.

In the wings, Lizzie could see Lady Azeena frantically signing to her assistant Bob. **'Rudy's disappeared!'**

Lizzie watched as Bob's mouth fell open in shock. Then he and Lady Azeena vanished into the darkness backstage.

Lizzie knew they must be looking for Rudy – and she and Lucky had to help! There was no time to waste – but they'd be even quicker if Ted helped too.

Lucky looked up at Lizzie as she pointed at Ted and made the sign for **'fetch'**. The puppy immediately raced over and brought Ted back to Lizzie, just as she'd been taught to do at home.

The three of them sprinted up the dark steps on the left of the stage behind the curtains. Different magicians and their assistants were milling around in the wings. Volunteer stagehands were busily working and Lizzie saw Dot struggling to carry the escapologist's giant sack. But there was no sign of Rudy anywhere. **Where could he be?**

'Trapdoor,' signed Ted.

'Houdini's hole!' signed Lizzie and Ted nodded, running off to look under the stage. Lizzie and Lucky headed in the opposite direction.

Although they had visited the theatre lots of time before, Lizzie and Lucky had never really explored it properly – there were so many nooks and crannies and hidden places. The theatre was old and had been constructed on an even older building that had been changed over the years. The rabbit could be anywhere!

Rudy had to be found and he had to be found quickly. But how and why had he disappeared in the first place?

When Lucky was just a tiny puppy,

she'd been stolen and Lizzie had rescued her. A magician's rabbit was probably worth a lot of money. Lizzie was worried that Rudy had been kidnapped by someone who wanted to hold him to ransom. She hoped he was safe. Lady Azeena needed him with her – she couldn't be a magician without him. They *had* to find him as soon as possible, because Lizzie knew only too well from her work as a detective that the trail would grow colder with every passing minute.

Then she noticed that one of the exit doors leading to the car park was open. There were lots of dangers outside for a missing rabbit, even a big one like Rudy – especially if he hadn't actually been taken but had run off because he'd been scared by something. There was traffic to worry about for a start. Dogs too – although Lucky was friendly, not all dogs were. And even if Rudy was spotted by a kind person, they probably wouldn't guess he was a magician's rabbit who'd escaped from the theatre. They might innocently decide to take him home and keep him.

Lizzie could now see Lady Azeena and Bob in the car park. It was the first place Lizzie would have looked too when she'd spotted the open door. Rudy could easily have scampered through it – straight into danger outside. Lady Azeena and her assistant were too busy searching beneath cars to notice Lizzie and Lucky. Bob was

lying on his stomach almost under one
of the vehicles.

Lizzie hoped Rudy was somewhere
inside and not out there.

Lucky had her nose down to the carpet,
sniffing around in different places. But
suddenly she looked up, sniffed at the air as
if she'd caught a scent of something – and
started running. Lizzie chased after her.

When they reached the props storage room, the puppy raced straight into it through the open door. Lizzie followed just as Dot came hurrying out, carrying the ornate old transformation magic box that had been empty one minute, then filled with jewels the next. Dot was so focused on carefully carrying the box that she almost bumped into Lizzie.

Lizzie wanted to ask her if she'd seen Rudy but Dot didn't know any sign language. Besides, she looked like she was busy.

Lizzie looked over at Lucky in one corner of the props room. She seemed to be scratching at something. The room was full of costumes, as well as the props the magicians had brought with them. Lizzie started searching under the costumes and behind the props, including the escapologist's giant sack she'd seen Dot carrying earlier.

Lucky came running over and dived head first into the sack, soon disappearing into it completely! Lizzie could see her doggy shape wriggling about.

Lizzie looked inside the opening of the bag to see what Lucky had found. The puppy was pulling at something with her teeth. Lizzie could feel that it was something soft. Between them, they pulled at the object, until Lucky eventually emerged backwards, dragging out the

velvet cushion that Rudy had been sitting
on!

What was it doing there?

An image suddenly flashed back
into Lizzie's head of Dot in the wings
struggling to hold the escapologist's sack!

Dot would have had more opportunity
than most people to steal Rudy. She was
one of the volunteer stagehands and could
go anywhere without suspicion. Lizzie had
seen her working the smoke machine, and

she remembered the shadow she'd seen darting about the stage. Had that been Dot stealing Rudy? Had she hidden Rudy inside the sack? But wouldn't she have needed someone else to help her? And why would Dot have taken Lady Azeena's rabbit?

Lucky was now following a trail of paw prints in a thin layer of green sand from a big sack that had fallen over. It looked very like the sand the wild professor magician had used in his act. Were they rabbit paw prints? They weren't the same as Lucky's. Lizzie took a closer look.

The paw prints led right into the sword cabinet – otherwise known as the blade box.

Lizzie was so focused on the paw prints in the green sand that she hadn't noticed what was happening in the background. She heard Lucky bark and then the next moment, someone shoved her from behind. Lizzie fell forward into the empty sword cabinet. The door banged shut and she was suddenly in darkness, apart from a few small gaps where the swords were supposed to go in.

She was trapped!

CHAPTER 8

Lucky barked and barked but Lizzie didn't come back. She didn't even open the door with the holes in it. Lucky sat down and whined but Lizzie still didn't come out. Lucky tilted her head from one side to the other, thinking about what she should do to help. She decided that she had to find Ted, so she jumped up and ran off to look for him.

*

Ted was under the stage in what was

called the trap room – because of the trapdoors – when Lucky came bounding up and gave a woof.

'What is it, Lucky?' Ted said and signed. 'Where's Lizzie?'

Lucky gave a quick wag of her tail before heading off with Ted right behind her. The puppy knew exactly where Lizzie was. Lucky ran along the corridor and round the corner. She looked up at Ted and then headed through the open props room door.

CHAPTER 9

Lizzie pushed at the door of the sword cabinet as hard as she could, but it didn't move. She tried to ignore the swirly feeling in her tummy. It was hard to breathe and she didn't like being trapped in the box at all. Lizzie shoved at the top and stamped on the bottom end of the cabinet, trying to find a weak spot. She *had* to get to Lady Azeena and let her know what had happened. **She had to save Rudy!**

Who had pushed her in here – and

why? Was it Dot? Lizzie was now convinced that the stagehand had hidden Rudy inside the magic transformation box she had been carrying as she left the props room. Dot must have concealed him in the escapologist's sack and then swapped him into the box. Rudy was a big rabbit and it would be easier to carry him around in the box than in an oversized bag. Plus it would look less suspicious. That's why the cushion had been in the sack! Dot must have taken it at the same time as she took Rudy. But *why* had she kidnapped the rabbit? The paw prints in the green sand looked just the right size to be Rudy's . . . which made Lizzie wonder whether the sand magician

108

had helped Dot snatch the rabbit.

Or *maybe* the sand magician was a red herring. Perhaps that's what the real criminal wanted her to think. The sand magician might just be a decoy, a way to misdirect her from the real criminal.

A trick!

It was possible that someone else entirely had taken Rudy. If that was the case, it had to be someone who knew the theatre well. Or at least someone who'd had the time to explore it.

Lizzie thought Mr O'Keith could definitely be a suspect. She wouldn't put anything past him. Plus she was sure he'd been lying about where the real theatre manager was. And what had he been saying to Dot and Ann when he was pointing at Lady Azeena? Were the three of them in cahoots to kidnap Rudy?

Lizzie suddenly remembered the sword-cabinet act she'd seen earlier and how the magician's assistant had vanished and then reappeared at the back of the theatre. Somehow, the assistant had escaped from the cabinet – but not through the front. *There had to be another way out.* A secret way through the back or the top or the sides of the cabinet.

Lizzie started to push again at each side of the box. The first side didn't move, and nor did the second. But there was a sheet of folded paper wedged into the third side. Lizzie pulled it out and put it in her pocket.

On the fourth side her fingers felt a tiny hook. Lizzie undid it, and the back of the cabinet swung open – she was finally free. She let out a long sigh of relief.

But where had Lucky gone? Lizzie headed out of the props room to try and find her. As she ran through the foyer, she saw Dot standing outside the theatre with Ann. The big transformation box was on the seat of her motorbike. Ann was opening her big Plant Pizza delivery bag. Dot opened the transformation box. Lizzie was sure they were about to put Rudy in the pizza bag. Once they had the rabbit inside it, the two girls could drive off on their motorbike with Rudy – and no one would know!

There was no time to waste. Lizzie couldn't let them get away with Rudy. She had to stop them. Lizzie dashed down the theatre steps.

When Dot saw her, she started shouting at Lizzie. It was hard for Lizzie to lipread because Dot's face was all contorted. But she understood this much:

'Help . . . terrible . . . Rudy!'

CHAPTER 10

'Rudy was right there in that box,' Dot said as Lizzie lipread. Dot pointed to the main part of the box lined with green and silver striped paper. 'But now he's gone!'

Lizzie gazed at the ornate container. It reminded her of a cardboard box with a silver paper mirror they'd once made at school during maths. It was much grander, but basically the same. *It's all to do with Pythagoras and mirrors*, the teacher had explained.

The old-looking transformation box was now open but there was no sign of Rudy inside. It just looked like an empty box lined with green and white stripes on the sides, top and bottom.

'Help us,' Ann said as Lizzie lipread.

'I only put it down for a minute,' said Dot. 'He can't have got out.'

Lizzie knew what to do and she knew how the vanishing trick box worked. It was all about mirrors and angles, she recalled. An illusion to do with triangles. What you saw wasn't really true. It was a reflection. Lots of magic tricks used mirrors.

Rudy wasn't in the main part of the box anymore. Somehow he'd got himself into the secret compartment on the top.

Only, to get to the hidden compartment, you didn't lift the lid from the front, as you would normally – but from the back. It wouldn't work any other way because that's how the transformation box had been built.

Lizzie lifted the lid from the back. It opened and, lo and behold, there was Rudy! Their excitement was short-lived, though. Something was wrong ... very wrong.

Rudy was lying on his back with his legs in the air.

Ann's scream was so loud Lizzie heard it and looked over at her.

'Is he dead?' Ann said.

Lizzie looked closely at the rabbit, felt

his pulse and shook her head. Rudy wasn't
dead, but she had to do something quickly.
Rudy had gone into a trance, and she
remembered Ted saying that it wasn't good
for a rabbit's heart. The only time they
played dead – due to tonic immobility –
was when they were held on their backs
and feared they were about to die.

The secret compartment was too small
to hold Rudy and he must have felt

trapped, just like Lizzie had in the sword cabinet. Then, as Dot carried him, being jolted around inside the box must have been too much for the frightened animal.

Rudy was in serious danger. Carefully, Lizzie lifted the rabbit out of the box so he wasn't lying on his back with his belly up anymore. She rested him against her and stroked him gently.

The air around them was tense and Lizzie was scared but tried to pretend she wasn't. She could feel so many eyes on her, but knew she needed to be calm and in control to help Rudy.

She continued to stroke him until, eventually, he gave a tiny shudder and came back to life. Lizzie gasped with relief and realized she'd been holding her breath.

She could see Dot and Ann's lips moving but she was too busy concentrating on Rudy to lipread what they were saying. Rudy's heart was now beating very fast but he was definitely much better than he had been before.

Lizzie smiled as Rudy opened his eyes and looked at her.

Just at that moment, Lucky came running out of the theatre, followed by Ted. Lucky started barking because she was so excited to see Lizzie. Ted's mouth opened and Lizzie saw him shouting **'Ruuuuuddddy!'**

Rudy jumped out of Lizzie's arms in fear and went racing up the steps and back into the theatre.

Lizzie, Ted, Dot and Ann ran after Rudy, but Lucky was quicker.

As Lizzie ran into the auditorium and down the aisle past the seats, she saw Rudy and Lucky scampering ahead of her towards the stage. Rudy hopped up the steps and Lucky ran straight after him. The two animals darted across the

stage from one side to the other, shocking
the balloon magicians who were in the
middle of their act and sending balloons
flying everywhere. Lizzie ran across
the stage after them and everyone else
followed in hot pursuit.

Mr O'Keith sprinted on to the stage in
an effort to catch the animals and stop
the chase. He tried to pounce on Rudy
but ended up on the wooden floor empty-
handed, chest down and very angry.

Then Lady Azeena came running from
the wings on the other side of the stage,
and with one giant leap Rudy flew into
her arms and she hugged him to her. The
magician had streaks of mascara running
down her face, but she was smiling from

ear to ear as she stroked Rudy and he snuggled into her. Safe at last.

Lucky gazed up at Lady Azeena and wagged her tail as if to say **You're welcome.**

'But what about your other animals? You don't even seem to care enough to give them some water,' Dot said to the magician, jabbing her finger out accusingly with each word. 'It's not right.'

Lady Azeena looked confused.

'It's cruel!' Ann shouted as Mr O'Keith tried to drag her away.

'Or not cruel?' Lizzie signed to Lady Azeena. 'Your act never was cruel really, was it? Lucky gave me the final clue.'

Lizzie signed the solution to the

mystery of the dangerous animals to Lady
Azeena.

Dot and Ann didn't understand because
they didn't know sign language. But Ted
did. He made the sign for **'Wow!'**

Lady Azeena gave a tiny nod to Lizzie
before putting a finger to her lips. It was
their secret . . . . for now.

CHAPTER 11

When Lizzie and Lucky got back to their
seat half an hour after they'd gone to help
Lady Azeena, they discovered that three
more seats had been put there.

'Mr O'Keith told us to bring them,' a
volunteer stagehand said.

'He also said to give you these,' said
another stagehand, holding out a great
big box of chocolates and a box of
popcorn from the theatre shop.

Lizzie was immediately suspicious.

What was the theatre manager up to now? Then she realized it could be another red herring. A way to stop her from investigating any further. Mr O'Keith was pretending he wasn't involved with Dot and Ann and the kidnapping of Rudy. But Lizzie had seen him whispering with the girls. Maybe they were all in it together.

Lizzie beckoned to Mum, Dad and Ted and they came hurrying over. Her parents told Lizzie how Mr O'Keith had announced that there would be a brief intermission after Lady Azeena had run off the stage. Mr O'Keith had also instructed the staff to make lots more complimentary popcorn to give out to people in the audience.

'Maybe he's not so bad after all,' Dad signed.

Lizzie wasn't sure about that. Not in the slightest! But she was very happy that Mum, Dad and Ted were now sitting with her and Lucky for the final act – **Astonishing Lady Azeena.**

Lucky happily pounced on her smiling

silver star toy when she spied it still lying on the floor waiting for her. Lizzie hoped Lucky wouldn't have chewed it too much by the time she gave it back to Lady Azeena. She was now certain it must be Rudy's toy, even though she hadn't actually seen the rabbit drop it.

Then the curtains opened and the spotlight shone on Rudy, sitting on his velvet cushion atop the small table once again. The carrot chew toy was under one of his paws. This time it was a lot less than thirty seconds before Lady Azeena appeared through the trapdoor in a puff of golden smoke.

Lucky, who'd jumped up into Lizzie's lap for a better view, looked over at her rabbit friend and gave a woof.

Lady Azeena's assistant, Bob, came to join her while Lady Azeena picked Rudy up and held him close. Rudy wriggled and she let him climb to her shoulder, where he sat like a pirate's parrot.

Lizzie and Ted started laughing. Rudy looked so sweet up there. The rest of the audience looked like they were laughing too.

Bob told the audience that Rudy was the sweetest but most stubborn rabbit Lady Azeena had ever had, and he loved doing tricks. But only when he felt like it! So now Rudy had lots of 'friends' to help him.

Then the trunks containing the dangerous wild animals were wheeled on to the stage. The padlocks were unlocked and the doors opened as the spectators held their breath.

The next moment, everyone **gasped** as four giant tarantulas came scuttling out and ran across the stage. They were followed by a python that hissed at the audience. Then more tarantulas ran on to the stage and were joined by a number of scorpions! Several screams echoed through the room.

Inside the trunks, as Lizzie had already worked out, were animals that didn't mind being in the dark or need to drink. For just a few moments, people were fooled. Then the ferocious creatures mingled with unicorns, dragons and dinosaurs.

The audience started to laugh heartily

when they realized the dangerous
creatures weren't actually real!

Dad frowned. 'So are they all . . .?'

Lizzie chuckled and nodded. 'None
of them are living, breathing animals –
apart from Rudy, of course. All of Lady
Azeena's animals are **robots and**

animatronic creatures!'

'The spiders and snakes and scorpions looked so real!' Ted signed.

Finally, a big mouse and a rabbit that looked very similar to Rudy came out.

Mum signed to Lizzie: 'Are they…?'

'Yes, they're robots too!' Lizzie signed back.

Rudy's 'friends' performed the tricks when Rudy decided he'd rather sit on Lady Azeena's shoulder and watch instead.

For the first trick, Rudy was supposed to appear out of a large wizard's hat, but when Lady Azeena pointed to the magical headwear, Rudy didn't move from her shoulder. Lady Azeena pointed again but Rudy still wouldn't budge.

Lady Azeena gave a theatrical sigh and showed the audience that the hat was empty. But in the next moment a large robot mouse leapt from it instead. The audience laughed and laughed. Lucky looked up at Lizzie with her head tilted to one side. **What was going on?**

Then Lady Azeena started to pull silk squares from her mouth and Rudy wanted to join in. Lucky became really excited and wanted to take part as well – this looked like a great game! She jumped off Lizzie's lap and went running past the audience, up the steps and on to the stage. Lizzie ran after her but didn't follow her onstage. She wasn't sure what to do. She didn't want to spoil Lady Azeena's

act. Rudy held one end of the string of
silk squares in his teeth – and then Lucky
snatched at it too, and the pair of them
pulled together. The audience clapped
delightedly.

Then Lady Azeena beckoned to Lizzie, who gingerly stepped up on to the stage.

Now everyone was applauding Lizzie and Lucky, and Mum, Dad and Ted were waving their hands in the air enthusiastically.

'Lady Azeena would be honoured if you would assist her,' Bob signed to Lizzie, pointing to a chair.

So Lizzie sat down. Lucky ran over and sat next to her, but Lizzie knew the puppy was very excited – even though she was trying to sit still, her tail kept wagging non-stop!

Lady Azeena put Rudy on the table next to Lizzie and made the sign for 'stay' to him. Next the magician picked up an enormous golden handbag and put it on the table – only for Rudy to stick his head inside when Lady Azeena wasn't looking. He emerged with Lady Azeena's oversized soft golden purse in his teeth.

Lady Azeena pretended to be confused as to where the purse had gone, which made the audience laugh even more.

Then there was the disappearing rabbit trick using mirrors and a fake – but very realistic – version of Rudy that looked almost exactly like him.

Then a fire-breathing robot dragon vanished from one place and reappeared in another, while Lucky went running after it, wanting to play. The python swapped places with a giant animatronic

spider ... and suddenly the fake animals –
and there were lots, including the dinosaur
and unicorn – were swapping places and
flying through the air as the performance
ended in a whirlwind of movement, with
all the creatures illuminated by spotlights.

Finally, Rudy, Lady Azeena, Lizzie and Lucky disappeared together in a thick cloud of smoke. The audience cheered delightedly and gave them a big round of applause.

All the magicians in the contest had performed brilliantly, but **Lady Azeena and her Amazing Animals** were the overall winners of the competition. The audience went wild as Lady Azeena was presented with the winner's trophy.

★

'I thought you were going to use real animals in your act. But actually it was only Rudy!' Ted signed to Lady Azeena in the green room afterwards. 'Plus a short appearance from Lucky.'

'That's what you were *supposed* to think. A magician's performance doesn't always start when the spotlight is turned on. Sometimes it begins long before then,' Lady Azeena told him.

'The quickness of the hand deceives the eye,' signed Lizzie.

She looked over at Dot and Ann. Mr O'Keith was talking to them, but his hand was in front of his mouth so she couldn't lipread what he was saying. Lizzie signed to Ted, 'What is he saying?' But Ted only shrugged and signed that Mr O'Keith was talking too quietly to hear.

The other contestants kept coming over to congratulate Lady Azeena. Ted showed them how to make the sign for **'congratulations'**.

★

Dot and Ann were desperate to talk to Lady Azeena.

'So no animals were ever going to be hurt?' they said. 'And you weren't being unkind, not letting them have a drink. In fact, having a drink could be very bad for them and stop them from working.'

Lady Azeena lipread and signed back to her assistant, Bob, who replied, 'Lady Azeena would never treat an animal

unkindly. She's seen too many animals
suffer over the years in the name of
entertainment. There's really no need for
it – not with what we can do today. And

people love Rudy, so he doesn't really have to do anything – just be here.'

'We only wanted to show you that the way we thought you were treating your animals was wrong,' Ann explained. 'But we were the ones who were wrong.'

'We thought taking your favourite animal would give you a shock. But we never wanted Rudy to get lost or hurt. We love animals and only want to help them. We wouldn't want to hurt one,' Dot added. 'Would we, Uncle Mickey?'

Mr O'Keith looked really embarrassed now.

'They're all related?' Lizzie signed to Ted, and Ted translated.

'Ann's my big sister,' said Dot and

Lizzie lipread. 'And Uncle Mickey's our mum's brother.'

'Dot got Uncle Mickey this job,' Ann said. 'She told Jenny she knew just the person to look after the theatre for the day. Jenny was desperate to find someone. It was really last minute.'

'I, um, I have had some experience before,' Mr O'Keith said. 'I knew what to do.'

Ann rolled her eyes. 'You mean you know how to boss people about!' she said.

Lizzie hid a smile. Mr O'Keith was very good at that! But if Dot had recommended him for the temporary job that meant he must have known what the girls were up to!

'Are you going to call the police?'

Mr O'Keith asked Bob, who signed the question to Lady Azeena.

'You don't have to – really you don't,' Ann and Dot said.

Lady Azeena didn't want the police involved.

'I'm sorry about my nieces – they're good girls really,' Mr O'Keith told Bob. 'And I'm sorry for the way I treated you and your puppy,' he told Lizzie. 'You'll both be more than welcome at the theatre any time and you can sit wherever you like. Jenny will be back tomorrow and I know she's very keen to welcome more pets into the theatre! She's at a meeting with other theatre managers from around the country today. They're discussing making theatres more dog friendly – as they're starting to do throughout the world in cinemas.'

Lizzie thought this was a very good idea. Her mum and dad were smiling too. Going to the cinema would be much more fun if Lucky could come as well – so long as the film had subtitles or an interpreter, like they'd had for the pantomime at this theatre.

She was also very glad Jenny was coming back tomorrow and that Mr O'Keith wouldn't be there. She still didn't trust him.

'Sometimes Uncle Mickey can be a real grump,' Ann laughed.

'This is for you,' Dot said, taking the

paw-print necklace from round her neck
and holding it out to Lizzie.

'Really?' signed Lizzie, and Dot nodded
and put it round Lizzie's neck.

'Looks good,' signed Ted.

Lizzie touched the necklace. She'd always liked it very much, but she didn't feel comfortable taking it. It didn't feel right.

Lizzie took the necklace off and gave it back to Dot, shaking her head.

'Dotty's really sorry for shoving you in the magician's blade box,' Ann said as Lizzie lipread.

Lizzie remembered the piece of paper she'd found wedged into the blade box side. She pulled it from her pocket and unfolded it. It was a

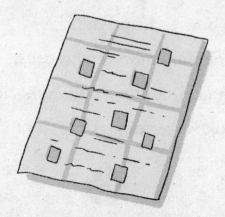

programme for the magic contest — but it had little squares cut out of it. **Why?**

'People should have more respect for paper,' Mr O'Keith said, scowling.

'We didn't know what to do about Rudy until you came along,' Ann said to Lizzie. 'But we have to go now.'

Lizzie watched as they hurried out of the door after their uncle.

★

'It was lucky you told me about tonic immobility,' Lizzie signed to Ted when they'd gone. 'Otherwise I wouldn't have known how to help Rudy.'

'It isn't only rabbits who get it,' Ted told her. 'Chickens do too, and even sharks if you stroke a certain spot under their chins!'

150

'I don't think I'd want to give that a try,' signed Lizzie's dad. Lizzie and Ted laughed and laughed because they wouldn't want to try it either.

Then Lucky wagged her tail at Rudy and dropped the smiling silver star toy in front of him.

'I'm sorry Lucky took Rudy's toy,' Lizzie signed, picking the star up and holding it out to Lady Azeena. 'I don't know where he found it. Rudy must have dropped it.'

Lady Azeena didn't take the toy from Lizzie. She shook her head. 'I've never seen it before,' she signed. 'It isn't Rudy's.'

Lizzie frowned. **Then whose could it be? It was a mystery.**

Lucky wagged her tail as Lizzie gave the toy back to her.

'My gran's never going to believe what happened here when I tell her,' Ted said, shaking his head.

And that gave Lizzie an idea.

CHAPTER

Ted's gran was very surprised when the golden stretch limousine stopped outside her house. She was even more surprised when Ted got out, followed by Lizzie and Lucky, then Lizzie's mum and dad. But her mouth fell open when she saw Lady Azeena emerge from the car with Rudy draped over her shoulder, followed by Bob.

'This is the *Amazing Lady Azeena*,' Ted said, introducing the magician to his gran, 'and Rudy the rabbit and Bob.'

Ted's gran looked like she couldn't
quite believe this was happening. 'How
– how do you do?' she burbled. She was
holding Lizzie's detective bag that she'd
left behind. Lizzie took it from her and
pulled out her phone. She took a photo

of the programme she'd found. There was

something she needed to do.

'Would you like to come for a short

drive?' Lady Azeena signed as Ted

translated for Gran.

It had been Lizzie's idea. She'd

thought that if anyone or anything could persuade Ted's gran to venture out of her house again, it would be a magician in a golden stretch limousine. No one could resist that!

Gran, however, looked a bit worried so Lizzie took her hand, smiled and nodded. Gran still didn't look too sure but she got in the car anyway. She sat next to the window, which was also Lucky's favourite place to sit. Lucky hopped up on to the old lady's lap.

'Get down, Lucky,' signed Lizzie. Even though the puppy wasn't very heavy, she was a bit worried that Lucky might be too heavy for Ted's gran.

But Gran shook her head. 'Let Lucky

stay. She's not being any bother and I like having her with me. You're a good pup, aren't you?'

Lucky gave Gran's face a delighted lick as the car set off.

Lady Azeena and Mum were sitting next to each other and busily signing and laughing. The Deaf world was small and they'd soon found that they had lots of mutual friends. Rudy perched on Lady Azeena's lap and watched them all.

Lizzie smiled when Ted's gran waved regally at her surprised neighbours as they drove past. Mrs Rose waved back, and Victor the golden Labrador wagged his tail.

Gran chuckled. 'I forgot how much fun

going out could be!' she said.

Lizzie looked out of the back window and saw Mrs Rose speaking on her phone.

'The inside of this car is even bigger than my room!' signed Ted.

'I expect the horn is loud,' signed Dad, which Ted translated to Bob, who was at the wheel of the limousine. Bob pressed his hand on the horn and gave it a long blast. The sound was loud enough for Dad to hear. Dad smiled and signed 'Lovely!'

★

Gran squeezed Lizzie's hand when they arrived back home after the fifteen-minute drive. **'Thank you,'** Lizzie lipread.

Dot and Ann were waiting by the gate

with Mrs Rose and Victor standing next
to them.

'I hope you don't mind me phoning
Dot and Ann to let them know you were
here,' Mrs Rose said and Ted translated.
'Ann gave me her mobile number. They're
so sorry for what happened.'

Lucky was really excited to see her
friend Victor. Once they'd bounded
through the back gate, the two dogs raced
up and down the garden and all around.

'Thank you again for persuading Mr O'Keith to let Lucky come into the theatre,' Lizzie signed to Mrs Rose.

Mrs Rose said it was her pleasure.

Dot had seen her trying to help Lizzie at the theatre and realized they must know each other. When the golden limousine had driven past her with Ted's gran in it, Mrs Rose had phoned Ann.

'We wanted to bring you something to say we're so sorry for what we did,' Dot said to Lady Azeena.

'My pizza place has the best strawberry ice cream,' Ann said as Ted translated. She was holding a giant-sized tub of it. 'I brought it as a peace offering.'

'There was just time for me to pick

160

some strawberries from my garden and
grab this bag of homemade sweet potato
chews before you got back – so everyone

can have something,' Mrs Rose said. 'I had a bumper crop of strawberries this year.'

Ted's gran wanted Dot and Ann to stay, but they said they had to go.

'Enjoy the ice cream,' said Ann.

'We really are truly sorry for what we did,' Dot said to Lady Azeena. 'We'll never do anything like that again. If there was a next time, we would inform the authorities if we thought there was animal abuse going on – and definitely *not* resort to kidnapping!'

Lady Azeena nodded as she stroked Rudy. The rabbit gazed at Dot and Ann and his nose twitched. He didn't seem frightened of them at all.

'I'll forgive you if you promise me you will always try to be kind and stand up for animals,' Lady Azeena signed to the sisters with a twinkle in her eye, while Bob translated.

'We promise,' they replied earnestly as Rudy nuzzled into Lady Azeena's neck.

'Uncle Mickey was wondering if you still had that programme with the missing letters?' Ann asked Lizzie just as they were leaving.

Lizzie lipread her and nodded.

'Uncle Mickey said he saw some actors chopping it up during one of their rehearsals for a play about blackmail,' Dot said. 'He said we should get it from you and give it back to the actors –

because they might need it as one of their props.'

Lizzie had an uneasy feeling. She suspected Dot and her sister may be lying, but she gave them the programme anyway.

'I don't trust Ann or Dot or their uncle,' Ted signed when they'd gone.

'Me neither,' signed Lizzie.

She took out her phone with the photo she'd taken of the cut-up programme on it. Ted pulled his full programme from his pocket. Now they could compare them. The squares turned out to be missing letters.

'O, m, a, s, r, n,' Lizzie read. What did that mean?

She grabbed a pen and paper from
her detective bag, wrote 'O m a s r n' at
the top and then started re-arranging the
letters. Everyone wanted to help.

'Man,' Lizzie wrote.

'Oar and soar,' signed Dad.

'I see the names Sam, Ron and Norm,' signed Mum.

'Moan,' said Gran.

'Roam,' signed Mrs Rose.

'Roma,' said Bob.

'Ram and ran,' signed Lady Azeena

'Mars,' signed Ted and suddenly Lizzie knew what it was.

*

'Ransom' she signed. The letters spelt ransom! It was the only word that used all the letters. Ann and Dot obviously knew more than they'd said about this – and so did their uncle. But why would Dot and Ann and their uncle need a ransom note if they weren't really kidnapping Rudy? Why would they need a ransom note if they were really animal lovers just trying to make a point?

Lady Azeena looked shocked. Mum squeezed her hand.

Dad made the sign for 'phone' and 'police' but Lady Azeena shook her head.

Whatever Dot and Ann and her uncle had intended to do, Rudy was safe and sound.

'That's all that matters,' Lady Azeena signed. 'That Rudy's safe.'

Lizzie nodded. Maybe kidnapping had always been Dot and Ann and their uncle's intention, or maybe they were animal lovers and it had all just got out of hand. Did they really love animals? They didn't seem to have worked with them before. Was that why they didn't know what had happened to Rudy when he got tonic immobility?

'Don't delete that photo,' Dad signed, pointing at Lizzie's phone.

Lizzie nodded. She was never going to delete it. It was evidence of both a possible crime and also evidence that not everyone is trustworthy.

'Forward it to me,' Lady Azeena signed and Lizzie did. Now, if Lady Azeena changed her mind about contacting the police, she'd have something to show.

'Keep doing your magic,' Lizzie said. 'You are amazing.'

And Lady Azeena nodded. 'I won't let this stop me,' she promised.

'Anyone for strawberries?' said Gran, when they'd all had time to think about what had happened. Everyone was surprisingly hungry.

'Houdini loved strawberries,' Dad signed. 'He had strawberries at his twenty-fifth wedding anniversary – *strawberry parfait* it was called. It's a bit like ice cream.'

'You know **everything** about Houdini, Dad,' Lizzie signed jokingly.

Ted took two strawberries upstairs for his rats, Jaws and Gobbler.

'Can Rudy have some lettuce?' Ted's gran asked Lady Azeena. Rudy was sitting on the sofa next to the magician.

'Oh yes, I think he'd like that very much,' Lady Azeena signed. So Gran gave him a leaf and Lizzie watched as Rudy nibbled.

Ted went out into the garden to give Thumper and Wriggles two strawberries, just as Victor and Lucky came running inside.

'One of the first things I taught Rudy was to come to me when I blew a whistle,' Lady Azeena signed to Lizzie.

'Just like a dog?' Lizzie signed back. Lucky always came when she blew the dog whistle. It didn't matter that Lizzie couldn't hear it – most hearing people couldn't either. 'Can rabbits hear as well as dogs?' she asked.

Lady Azeena shook her head but she was smiling as she signed in reply. 'No, rabbits can hear **even better** than dogs!'

'What about their sense of smell? That can't be as good as a dog's, can it?' Ted asked, coming back from feeding Thumper and Wriggles.

'A rabbit's sense of smell is up to twenty times better than that of a human,' Lady Azeena signed to him. 'It is so good that they can smell food from two miles away! It's as good as a dog's, but different.'

Just then, Lucky and Victor trotted over to see what tasty food was on offer. Mrs Rose gave them a sweet-potato chew each. 'They're Victor's favourites,' she said.

Lizzie looked at the dribble running from Victor's mouth and signed that she could tell!

'I'm glad you have two rabbits,' Lady

Azeena signed to Ted. 'It's better for rabbits not to live alone. They like company. Rudy is my only rabbit at the moment but he has his cat friend, Horace. They like cuddling up on the sofa and watching TV with me.'

Ted's eyes opened wide.

'I'd love to have Thumper and Wriggles indoors watching TV with me!'

'But your rabbits aren't toilet-trained like Rudy,' said Ted's gran, pulling a face. 'I don't want to keep finding lots of messes.'

Lady Azeena laughed. 'Toilet-training rabbits couldn't be simpler,' she signed. 'It's as easy as training a dog or a cat – easier, in fact. Rabbits like to eat and go to the toilet at the same time, so I have a hay rack next to Rudy's litter tray for him to nibble on. He always goes where he's supposed to!'

Victor was now snoozing, but Lucky was staring intently at Thumper and Wriggles's hutch through the window. Lizzie watched her and frowned. What was so interesting out there?

Then Lucky jumped up and gave a bark, waking Victor up.

Lizzie's eyes followed what Lucky had seen – Thumper and Wriggles were escaping from their hutch yet again! The door was now open and the rabbits had **jumped,** one after the other, on to the ground below. Lizzie wasn't sure if they'd managed to push the bolt open with their paws, or if the bolt was loose and they'd just pushed against the door.

'I hope they don't get into your garden,' Ted said to Mrs Rose.

'Well, they can't escape any further if they do,' Mrs Rose said. 'And they do love eating my strawberries. I've seen them nibbling on them a few times now.'

'Rabbits love lots of different fruits and herbs,' signed Lady Azeena. 'But most of them don't like lavender.'

Thumper and Wriggles didn't even try to get into Mrs Rose's garden today. They nibbled on the carrot tops Lizzie had tied to the low branches. Then Thumper started scrabbling in the digging spot Ted had made. The rabbits looked excited and happy. They were having fun!

Ted grabbed Lizzie's arm as Thumper went running excitedly across the grass and suddenly leapt up and spun round

180 degrees in mid-air. Ted made the sign for **'Gobsmacked!'** Thumper had done a binky!

A second later, Wriggles went running after Thumper and leapt into the air mid-run and did a binky too.

Lizzie grinned at Ted and he grinned back as they headed outside. It looked like the rabbit adventure garden plan had worked!

The rabbits were really enjoying themselves, but finally Ted decided they should return to their hutch.

'I'm going to make it bigger – **much bigger,**' he said. 'Rabbits should have lots of space.'

Lizzie nodded and helped him to catch Thumper and Wriggles. But she gasped as she put Thumper back inside. What was Lucky's toy octopus doing inside the hutch? Surely the rabbits couldn't have taken it? Or could they? It was a mystery. Just like the silver star toy. Lizzie knew that as good a detective as she was, there would always be some mysteries that she could never solve. And she wouldn't put anything past clever rabbits Thumper and Wriggles!

Lucky came running out of the house as soon as the door was opened for her. She didn't like being away from Lizzie for long. Lucky was very pleased to see her octopus toy again and gave it a big shake.

When Thumper saw Lucky, though, she thumped her foot on the floor of the hutch, as usual, warning the puppy to keep her distance.

★

They spent the next hour enjoying the delicious food and when it was time for the guests to leave, Lady Azeena signed to Lizzie, 'Thank you once again – I don't know what I would have done without your help in solving Rudy's disappearance.'

'Houdini made an elephant disappear once,' Dad signed. 'He did it in front of thousands of people and no one ever knew how.'

Ted signed, 'I bet Lizzie would have worked out how Houdini did it.'

Lizzie had a very good idea of how the disappearing elephant illusion could have been done. It was all to do with mirrors.

In magic things weren't always what they seemed – just like people weren't always what they seemed.

Lady Azeena smiled at Lizzie. 'You really are extremely good at solving mysteries.'

'That's because Lizzie and Lucky are the best detectives and mystery solvers in

181

the whole world!' signed Ted.

Lizzie laughed and Lucky gazed up at her and wagged her tail. 'Maybe not the **whole** world,' Lizzie signed back. But she was looking forward to whatever their next mystery might be.

THE END

THANK YOU

Hey presto!

Books don't just appear like magic. Many other people, besides me, were involved in getting this story to you. I would like to thank the talented 'magicians' who helped me to create this book and make it available for you to read. Fanfare please for:

Sara Jafari and Katie Sinfield, editors extraordinaire. Copy-editor and sign-language user Pippa Shaw, plus Mary O'Riordan. Proof reader Stephanie

Barrett. And my lovely agent and friend, Clare Pearson.

The dazzling illustrations of Tim Budgen and the designers, Arabella Jones and Janene Spencer.

Publicist Lily Orgill, magical marketer Michelle Nathan, and the spell-binding sales team of Rozzie Todd, Toni Budden and Kat Baker, who all worked so hard on the sales – thank you all very much.

The idea for *The Mystery of the Disappearing Rabbit* began when I heard about the World Deaf Magician's Festival. This led me to American magician and writer Simon Carmel, who told me how the great Houdini had learnt to fingerspell in both American and British sign languages. Thumbs up to Houdini!

My husband, Eric, especially enjoyed helping with the research for this book. We watched lots of magicians and gasped at their amazing tricks.

Eric also took our golden retrievers, Freya and Ellie, for long walks while I was busy signing in online meetings. (Freya and Ellie always wanted to go to the river, where they rolled in non-magical smelly stuff and then went swimming to wash it off.)

Prior to writing this book I hadn't realized how absolutely amazing rabbits are – just like all animals. Reading about therapy rabbits touched my heart. But I'm also much more aware now, thanks to the Rabbit Welfare Association, of rabbits' need for space and enrichment. Please do support their 'A Hutch is not Enough' campaign if you can.

I'm very excited that the first Lizzie and Lucky book is being translated into British Sign Language. Thank you so much to the RAD and for the support of the Arts Council and many sign-language-using friends. BSL is such a beautiful language and I want to share it with as many people as possible.

Finally, thanks to you for reading this book. I hope you enjoy it and may all your wildest wishes come true.

Megan

HOW TO KEEP YOUR BUNNY HAPPY

Want to know how to properly care for your rabbit? Here are some key steps:

1. Give them lots of love

Rabbits are friendly animals, so be sure to give them lots of attention and love. They love making friends and being sociable!

2. Treat them with care

Be careful when holding your bunny. Be sure not to lay them on their back or pick them up by their ears as it can harm them.

$\longrightarrow$

3. Give them yummy, bunny-friendly treats!

As well as hay and rabbit food from the pet shop, rabbits also need fruit and vegetables to complete their diet. They love chewing anything, so also make sure to also cover all electric wires in your house or your rabbit might nibble on them, which could be very dangerous!

4. Train them

Rabbits are smart – they love to think and cross obstacles. Cardboard castles are always helpful to excite your bunny. You can also train them so a specific area in their pen can be designated for their toilet area.

5. Pamper them

Rabbits love to take care of their fur, but they (sometimes) need your help. So be sure to gently brush their fur to get rid of insects and keep their fur clean and shiny.

6. Give them a big enough space to hop freely!

Your bunny is curious and loves moving around. The world is their playground! As they are highly social and territorial about their space, rabbits love to roam around their own house, and need enough room to do so.

7. Give them company

Rabbits love company, are highly social creatures and love being in a pair. They enjoy being in the company of other rabbits, so if you can, give your rabbit a friend to live with!

8. Be quiet

Sudden movements can scare rabbits – so be careful not to be too loud or move too quickly around your furry friend!

LEARN TO SIGN

Can you read the dedication at the front
of the book using sign language?

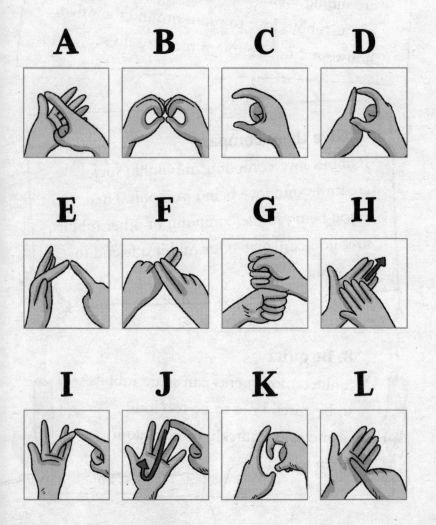

A B C D

E F G H

I J K L

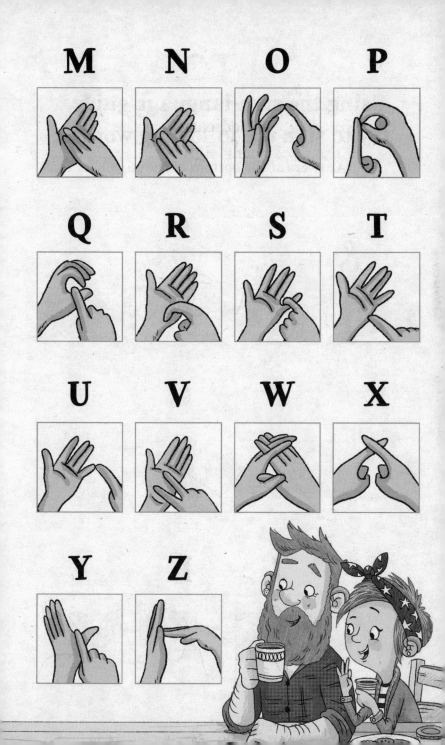

Using the sign-language guide, try to sign the following words:

(Answers at the bottom of the page.)

R _ _ _ _ _

_ _ _ _

_ _ _ _

4 _____ _____ _____ _____

5 _____ _____ _____ _____ _____

6 _____ _____ _____ _____ _____ _____

7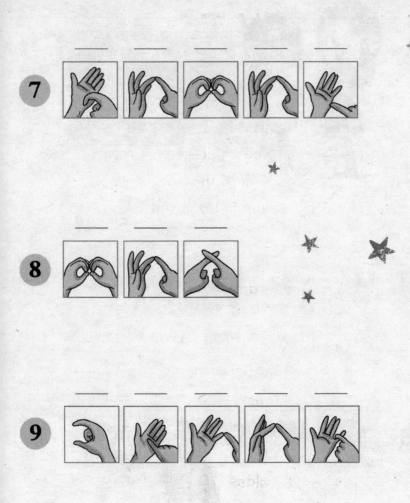
_____   _____   _____   _____   _____

8
_____   _____   _____

9
_____   _____   _____   _____   _____

HOW TO BE A DETECTIVE

Feeling inspired by Lizzie and Lucky, and want to be a detective yourself?

First, you need the equipment.

This is what's inside Lizzie's detective bag:

- Torch
  (or a torch on a mobile phone)
- Phone
- Clue bag
- Notebook and pencil
- Detective gloves
  (any kind of gloves to protect your hands)
- Tweezers
- Magnifying glass

Next, you need to dress the part.
Wear clothes that help you blend in —
plain clothes would work well!

Then, in your notebook, begin
writing things you notice about
your surroundings. Every detective
has a keen eye — that means they
observe everything around them.
Maybe look outside your window
and note down everything you see.

You can use your torch to inspect dark
areas, perhaps under the sofa or your bed
— you never know what you might find!
If you see anything suspicious, use your
tweezers to carefully pick it up and put it
inside your clue bag. $\longrightarrow$

You could even go outside to investigate further. Are there any footprints on the floor? Any trails of mud? Does anything look different to normal? Use your magnifying glass to really inspect the things around you. And note down your findings.

Once you've done this, you're well on your way to becoming a detective – your next step is to piece together your clues and find a mystery to solve …

Loved this book? Check out Lizzie & Lucky on their other adventures!

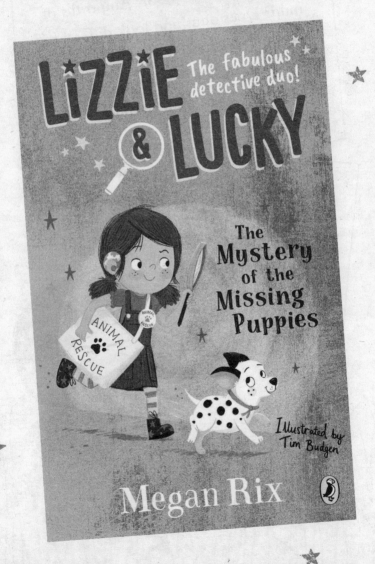

Lizzie The fabulous
detective duo!

& LUCKY

The
Mystery
of the
Stolen
Treasure

ANIMAL

Illustrated by
Tim Budgen

Megan Rix